Praise for Ra
and his Pastor Stephe

"Keating has accumulated an impressive assortment of characters in his series, and he gives each of them ample opportunity to shine... As in the preceding novels, the author skillfully blends Grant's sermonizing with intermittent bouts of violence. It creates a rousing moral quandary for readers to ponder without either side overwhelming the storyline. Tight action scenes complement the suspense (uncertainty over when the next possible attack will be) ... The villains, meanwhile, are just as rich and engrossing as the good guys and gals. The familiar protagonist, along with sensational new and recurring characters, drives an energetic political tale."

- *Kirkus Reviews* on *Reagan Country*

"First-rate supporting characters complement the sprightly pastor, who remains impeccable in this thriller."

- *Kirkus Reviews* on *Lionhearts*

"A first-rate mystery makes this a series standout..."

- *Kirkus Reviews* on *Wine Into Water*

"The author packs a lot into this frantically paced novel... a raft of action sequences and baseball games are thrown into the mix. The multiple villains and twists raise the stakes... Stephen remains an engaging and multifaceted character: he may still use, when necessary, the violence associated with his former professions, but he at least acknowledges his shortcomings—and prays about it. Action fans will find plenty to love here, from gunfights and murder sprees to moral dilemmas."

- *Kirkus Reviews* on *Murderer's Row*

Murderer's Row was named KFUO's BookTalk "Book of the Year" in 2015.

The River was a 2014 finalist for KFUO's BookTalk "Book of the Year."

"Ray Keating is a great novelist."

- host of KFUO radio's BookTalk

"A gritty, action-stuffed, well-considered thriller with a gun-toting clergyman."

- *Kirkus Reviews* on *The River*

"President Ronald Reagan's legacy will live on in the U.S., around the world and in the pages of history. And now, thanks to Ray Keating's *Reagan Country*, it will live on in the world of fiction. *Reagan Country* ranks as a page-turning thriller that pays homage to the greatest president of the twentieth century."

- Tom Edmonds, producer of
the official documentary on President Reagan,
Ronald Reagan: An American President

"Mr. Keating's storytelling is so lifelike that I almost thought I had worked with him when I was at Langley. Like the fictitious pastor, I actually spent 20 years working for the U.S. intelligence community, and once I started reading 'The River,' I had to keep reading because it was so well-crafted and easy to follow and because it depicted a personal struggle that I knew all too well. I simply could not put it down."

- Kenneth V. Blanchard
The Washington Times review of *The River*

"Must read for any Reaganite."

- Craig Shirley,
Reagan biographer and presidential historian,
on *Reagan Country*

"I miss Tom Clancy. Keating fills that void for me."

- *Lutheran Book Review* on
Murderer's Row

"Ray Keating has a knack for writing on topics that could be pulled from tomorrow's headlines. An atheist mayor-elect of NYC? I could envision that. Pastor Grant taking out a terrorist? I could see that."

- *Lutheran Book Review* on *An Advent for Religious Liberty*

"Thriller and mystery writers have concocted all manner of main characters, from fly fishing lawyers to orchid aficionados and former ballplayers, but none has come up with anyone like Stephen Grant, the former Navy Seal and CIA assassin, and current Lutheran pastor. Grant mixes battling America's enemies and sparring with enemies of traditional Christian values, while ministering to his Long Island flock. The amazing thing is that the character works. The Stephen Grant novels are great reads beginning with *Warrior Monk*, which aptly describes Ray Keating's engaging hero."

- David Keene, former American Conservative Union chairman, former National Rifle Association president, and former opinion editor at *The Washington Times*

"*Root of All Evil?* is an extraordinarily good read. Only Ray Keating could come up with a character like Pastor Stephen Grant."

- Paul L. Maier, author of *A Skeleton in God's Closet, More Than A Skeleton,* and *The Constantine Codex*

"*Warrior Monk* by Ray Keating has all of the adventure, intrigue, and believable improbability of mainstream political thrillers, but with a lead character, Pastor Stephen Grant, that resists temptation."

- *Lutheran Book Review* on *Warrior Monk*

Marvin Olasky, editor-in-chief of WORLD magazine, lists Ray Keating among his top 10 Christian novelists.

Heroes & Villains

A Pastor Stephen Grant Short Story

Ray Keating

Blessings!
Ray Keating

This book is a work of fiction. Names, characters, places, events and incidents either are the product of the author's imagination or are used fictitiously. Any resemblance to actual persons, living or dead, events or locales is entirely coincidental.

For more information:
Keating Reports, LLC
P.O. Box 596
Manorville, NY 11949
raykeating@keatingreports.com

ISBN-10: 1718881614
ISBN-13: 978-1718881617

Cover design by Tyrel Bramwell.

For my Heroes -
Jonathan,
David
and
Beth

Previous Books by Ray Keating

Reagan Country: A Pastor Stephen Grant Novel (2018)

Lionhearts: A Pastor Stephen Grant Novel (2017)

Wine Into Water: A Pastor Stephen Grant Novel (2016)

Murderer's Row: A Pastor Stephen Grant Novel (2015)

The River: A Pastor Stephen Grant Novel (2014)

An Advent for Religious Liberty:
A Pastor Stephen Grant Novel (2012)

Root of All Evil? A Pastor Stephen Grant Novel (2012)

Warrior Monk: A Pastor Stephen Grant Novel (2010)

In the nonfiction arena...

Unleashing Small Business Through IP:
The Role of Intellectual Property in Driving
Entrepreneurship, Innovation and Investment
(Revised and Updated Edition, 2016)

Unleashing Small Business Through IP:
Protecting Intellectual Property, Driving Entrepreneurship
(2013)

Discussion Guide for Warrior Monk:
A Pastor Stephen Grant Novel (2011)

"Chuck" vs. the Business World: Business Tips on TV
(2011)

U.S. by the Numbers:
What's Left, Right, and Wrong with America State by State
(2000)

New York by the Numbers:
State and City in Perpetual Crisis (1997)

D.C. by the Numbers: A State of Failure (1995)

"I have fought the good fight, I have finished the race, I have kept the faith."

- 2 Timothy 4:7

"The only real politics I knew was that if a guy liked Hitler, I'd beat the stuffing out of him and that would be it."

- Jack Kirby

"Doesn't matter what the press says. Doesn't matter what the politicians or the mobs say. Doesn't matter if the whole country decides that something wrong is something right. This nation was founded on one principle above all else: The requirement that we stand up for what we believe, no matter the odds or the consequences. When the mob and the press and the whole world tell you to move, your job is to plant yourself like a tree beside the river of truth, and tell the whole world – 'No, you move.'"

- Captain America,
as written by J. Michael
Straczynski in *Civil War:
The Amazing Spider-Man*

"Blessed are those who are persecuted for righteousness' sake, for theirs is the kingdom of heaven."

- Matthew 5:10

Brief Dossiers on Recurring Characters

Pastor Stephen Grant. After college, Grant was a Navy SEAL and then worked at the CIA. He subsequently became a Lutheran pastor, serving at St. Mary's Lutheran Church on the eastern end of Long Island. Grant grew up in Ohio, just outside of Cincinnati. He possesses a deep knowledge of theology, history, and weapons. His other interests include archery, golf, writing, movies, the beach, poker and baseball, while also knowing his wines, champagnes and brews. Stephen Grant is married to Jennifer Grant.

Jennifer Grant. Jennifer is a respected, sought-after economist. Along with Yvonne Hudson and Joe McPhee, she is a partner in a consulting firm. Her first marriage to then-Congressman Ted Brees ended when the congressman had an affair with his chief of staff. Jennifer loves baseball (a Cardinals fan while her husband, Stephen, cheers on the Reds) and literature, and has an extensive sword and dagger collection. Jennifer grew up in the Las Vegas area, with her father being a casino owner.

Pastor Zackary Charmichael. Zack is the assistant pastor at St. Mary's Lutheran Church. He grew up in the state of Washington, is a comic-book and gaming nerd, and a big fan of Seattle's Mariners and Seahawks as well as hockey's Canucks. Zack is married to Cara, who is a nurse.

Chapter 1

A deep, gravelly voice stated, “My plan simply makes more sense.”

Listening on the other end of the call, it was clear that the man was working to sound confident, but his quivering was unmistakable. “Hey, you work for me. I’m hiring you.”

“Yes, you are. You’re paying me a lot of dough. I have an obvious investment in making this a success. Each of us needs to get what we want. That includes not getting me and my team caught or even killed.”

Exasperation could be heard over the phone. “Yes, yes, of course.”

“Also, I’ve done this before. That’s why you’re paying me.”

“Yes, yes, of course. But why is yours the best option? Why not what I said when we first spoke?”

“Think about it. Your way leads back to you. That’s the most obvious outcome.”

“And your way won’t?”

“No. Again, think for a moment. Why would it? It’s clean. No evidence. No one to question. And obviously no one to renege on any deal. And as they say, ‘No body, no crime.’”

“I don’t like it.”

“What’s not to like?”

“It’s too much, too harsh.”

A trace of annoyance could now be detected in the gravelly voice. “Hey, this is dirty business. If you don’t have the stomach for it, then why did you contact me in the first place? You told me this has to happen. If not, well, I don't appreciate having my time wasted."

"Yes, yes, of course. Unfortunately, the fool will probably never change. He can't see what's in front of him; he's reactionary."

"Does that mean I have the green light for my plan?"

The nervous quivering still lingered. "He'll get one more chance. Depending on that, I'll make the call, and you'll be paid accordingly."

Chapter 2

Jennifer Grant observed, "This is completely new territory."

Stephen Grant replied, "I'm sure it will be fine."

"Hmmm. I don't know. Are you sure you're ready for this?"

He laughed, and said, "Yes. I'm actually looking forward to it."

She smiled in response.

It was early on a Friday night, and the two were sitting at the island bar in their kitchen. Stephen was sipping from a glass of iced tea, while Jennifer was finishing a cup of hot Earl Grey.

"Zack is excited about tonight and the weekend, while at the same time being disappointed that Cara had to cancel at the last minute."

"I know. But with the flu sweeping through the hospital, she had no choice."

He nodded and took another swig of tea.

Jennifer added, "And now, you're pinch hitting for his wife."

"I guess."

"Well, how could he be disappointed with that?"

Stephen smirked, and said, "Good point."

Jennifer glanced at the clock on the wall. "Alright, my love, I'm going to leave." Jennifer slipped off a kitchen stool, kissed her husband on the cheek, and took her cup to the sink. "I'm picking up Joan."

"Enjoy dinner and the movie."

"I will, and I hope you enjoy your first comic book convention."

"Ah, actually, Best's Long Island Comic-Con is a comic book, science fiction and fantasy gathering, and tonight is only the awards dinner. The con gets rolling tomorrow."

"Right, how could I forget? And did you just say 'the con'?"

"I most certainly did."

Jennifer smiled again and shook her head. "And you're really going dressed like that?"

"Wow. Isn't that one of those questions only asked when married too long?"

"You know what I mean. I'm pretty sure you're going to be the only one in clericals."

"The dinner is a jacket-and-tie affair. So, I'm actually being a bit of a rebel going with jacket and collar. You know, counter-cultural."

"Your boldness is one of the reasons I love you. And Zack is okay with this?"

Stephen enjoyed this kind of fun banter with his wife. "I don't have to check with Zack in terms of what I'm wearing. I'm a grown man who was with the Navy SEALs and the CIA."

Jennifer crossed her arms and raised an eyebrow.

Stephen continued, "Yeah, he said it would be fine. In fact, he's wearing his as well, since we've been in them all day anyway."

Stephen Grant was the senior pastor at St. Mary's Lutheran Church, with Zack being the assistant pastor at the parish.

"Okay, have fun. See you later."

"Wait." Stephen hopped off his stool, walked over and slipped his arms around his wife. Her short, auburn hair, sharp facial features but with a slightly upturned nose, and thin body were so familiar, and yet always so engrossing. He looked into her brown eyes and said, "You look beautiful." They kissed, and he added, "I love you."

Jennifer said, “Love you, too.” She took a deep breath while looking back into Stephen’s green eyes, and said, “You’re not so bad yourself, but now I really have to go.”

“Yes, me, too.”

Jennifer drove down the driveway in her Mojave Sand-colored, four-door Jeep Wrangler. A few minutes later, Stephen followed in his new blue Chevy Tahoe.

Chapter 3

Stephen didn't have to get out of his SUV after pulling into the driveway of St. Mary's parsonage. Zack Charmichael immediately stepped out of the house, locked the front door, and bounded to the Tahoe.

Zack jumped into the front passenger seat. While closing the door and locking his seatbelt, he said, "Hi, Stephen. Thanks again for driving."

"Glad to do it. How's Cara?"

"I think she's more disappointed about how I feel that she's not going. She enjoys some of this stuff – in particular, the sci-fi – but I think she just feels bad about not being able to be there to share my enthusiasm. At the same time, though, she's glad you're going in her place."

"Enthusiasm" is the right word, thought Grant.

The five-foot-seven-inch, wiry Zack Charmichael recently groomed a new look. That included neatly cut brown hair, the addition of a beard and mustache, and dark, rectangular glasses. Combined with the clergy attire, Stephen noted that Zack did manage to look, well, more mature. But Stephen also reflected that Zack's passing 30 years of age, getting married, and becoming a good pastor might have more to do with the maturity thing, rather than his hair and beard. At the same time, Stephen was glad that Zack showed no signs of losing his enthusiastic outlook for life, the Church and his varied interests, including comic books and science fiction.

"It's great that you guys enjoy sharing each other's interests," Stephen commented.

"It's cool. I'm looking forward to going with her next month to a Wolfe Pack event."

"Wolfe Pack?"

"It's the literary society for Rex Stout's Nero Wolfe mysteries. Cara loves mysteries, and she introduced me to Stout's Nero Wolfe books. They rank among her favorites, and I've come to like them, too."

"Okay, I'll put Nero Wolfe on my to-be-read list. Wasn't there a TV show?"

"Yeah. Cara has it on DVD if you want to borrow it."

"Sounds good."

Zack then switched gears to the dinner event they were heading to now. "I'm still surprised that I was able to get tickets for tonight, not to mention Best's Long Island Comic-Con is happening so close by." The Suffolk Arena was only two exits away on the Long Island Expressway from St. Mary's.

"Tell me more about the author who is receiving a lifetime achievement award tonight?"

"Wes Jenkins. He ranks as one of the great storytellers, as a writer and artist, in comic book history."

Stephen noted that Zack was ramping up the enthusiasm to provide the Jenkins' bio.

Zack continued, "Early on, he had great runs with some of the big DC and Marvel characters. But then he teamed up with Simon Huck to form J&H Comics Publishing. Fans and people in the industry thought Jenkins was nuts. No one predicted his subsequent burst... No, wait, 'burst' doesn't capture it. No one predicted his outbreak or storm of creativity. He gave comic book fans dozens of heroes and villains, ranging from more classic, bright characters to dark, noir-ish ones. Jenkins' creativity, coupled with Huck's eye for bringing in complementary talent, launched J&H from nowhere to the third largest comics house."

"Impressive."

"You'll appreciate the fact that Jenkins' work is rich in biblical allegories, and Greek and Roman myths. He also likes to play with historical parallels."

"Count me intrigued." Grant turned onto the Long Island Expressway entrance ramp. "So, tonight's awards dinner is, in part, a salute to an industry great."

"Yes and no."

"Why 'no'?"

"Well, Jenkins wrote a piece not too long ago in *The Wall Street Journal* challenging much of the comic book industry's hard Left turn in recent years."

"Left turn?"

"Some of the management and a good chunk of the creators now seem more interested in being social justice warriors – or SJWs – than telling great stories. That's meant a descent into moral relativism and ambiguity, political correctness, anti-Americanism, and an anti-Christian bent."

"Moral relativism in superhero comics? How does that work?"

Zack nodded. "I know. The very definition of the genre is a battle between good and evil. But there's been a big ramping up in left-wing preaching, including altering some longtime characters to fit that agenda, and a growing hostility toward political opponents, idealism and, of course, patriotism. Jenkins argued that this hasn't been a case of expanding viewpoints in comics, but instead an SJW push to silence more conservative voices. His view is backed up by assorted social media rants from some of the newer creators. They're not shy in making it clear that they hate anyone who disagrees with their liberal politics. In their books, assorted villains spew these bizarre political diatribes that amount to putting a murderous spin on whatever the Left disagrees with."

"Ah, so, the Stalinist Left has reached into the world of comic books."

Zack whipped his head in Stephen's direction. "Jenkins used that phrase – 'Stalinist Left' – in his article."

Stephen smiled, and said, "Well, great minds..."

Zack laughed, and replied, "Yeah, right. If that's what you need to hear."

"The point is that there tends to be a Stalin-esque impulse on the Left to silence opposing views. Of course, Stalin took that to the most extreme. But in general, the Left is very intolerant of, well, any kind of disagreement."

Zack said, "But this isn't the old Soviet Union."

"No. But a strain of this thinking has been present on college campuses since the Sixties. Many people point to the influence of Herbert Marcuse, a kind of godfather of the New Left, who claimed that since there can be no *real* free speech outside a Marxian society, freedom had to be opposed, even suppressed. Turning freedom on its head, he argued against freedom of thought in the name of a freedom that actually turned out to be nothing more than despotism by so-called enlightened intellectuals."

"Ugh. The Sixties were screwy."

"Yeah, and we're still paying the price today. Of course, the severity of the leftist reaction intensifies with the perceived threat, which is why Christianity gets so harshly treated."

"Jenkins' argued much of that. He also pointed out that comics always have had something to say about society and people, but talented storytellers did so in a way that the readers weren't hit over the head with a two-by-four and explicitly told what they were supposed to think."

"Sounds like Jenkins didn't pull any punches."

"He didn't, but it was important for someone of his stature to say these things."

Stephen asked, "Given his stance, what kind of reception is Jenkins going to receive tonight when he's handed his award?"

"Not sure. My guess is that he'll get a standing ovation from the section with fan tables where we'll be sitting. As for the tables with industry people, who knows?"

"Hmmm."

Zack asked, "What is it?"

"I'm reminded of when director Elia Kazan received a lifetime achievement Oscar in 1999, and the reaction among Hollywood luminaries ranged from remaining seated and not applauding, to staying seated and applauding, to standing and clapping."

"What was up with Kazan?"

"He was a great director, without a doubt. His films include *On the Waterfront*, *Viva Zapata!*, *A Streetcar Named Desire*, *East of Eden*, *Gentleman's Agreement*, the list goes on. But he had the nerve, in Hollywood's view at least, to oppose the communists infiltrating the movie business, especially labor unions, in the forties and fifties. The Left to this very day, of course, views that as an unforgiveable sin." Stephen exited the expressway, and guided his Tahoe toward the arena's parking lot.

Zack observed, "The comparison works. Any kind of opposition to or disagreement with the social justice warriors in comics is not tolerated and punished accordingly – again, especially online."

"How long has this been going on?"

"Jenkins argues that it started in the mid-2000s, but it really shifted into high gear over the last eight years."

"So, how has Jenkins continued to work?"

"His reputation still matters, to some extent. But like I said, he and Huck started up their own publishing house. And tons of fans love his stories, art, and creations, and aren't looking to get hit over the head with lefty propaganda."

"Fair enough."

"I hope J&H stands firm."

"Why wouldn't it?"

"It should. Simon Huck recently retired, and handed over his editor and publisher roles to Drake Werth. I don't know much about Werth, but I assume he's in line with Huck and Jenkins."

Stephen pulled his SUV into a parking spot.

Zack continued, "As a comics fan, this entire trend has been pretty discouraging. It's quite a change from a time not that long ago when, according to Jenkins, no one in the comics industry really knew or cared much about a creator's politics. The focus was on good storytelling."

"It's not unique to comic books. So many aspects of life have been politicized, from education to sports. Remember when Americans, no matter what their political beliefs, could sit down and watch a football game together?"

"Yeah. This entire thing sucks."

Stephen nodded. "It does, and it all has a Stalinist, or at least Marcuse, flavor."

"But you know what?"

"What?"

Zack smiled broadly. "I don't care about any of that right now. I'm looking forward to this dinner, and seeing Wes Jenkins get his award."

"Good. Let's go inside," concluded Stephen.

Chapter 4

The awards dinner was held in one of the rooms of the convention hall attached to the arena. A microphone and lectern stood at the front of the space. Assorted people working in the comic book business were seated at seven tables closest to the lectern, with another 20 tables of mainly fans beyond.

The initial reaction to the lifetime achievement award for Wes Jenkins went according to Pastors Grant and Charmichael's expectations. As Jenkins was being handed the award, the responses in the front seven tables were mixed, while the fans cheered and stood.

As Jenkins approached the lectern, Stephen was struck by how mild-mannered the man looked, with a thick head of black hair, a long face, large glasses, a crooked smile, large ears, and an average build with a slight stomach paunch. In a folksy, Midwestern tone, Wes Jenkins went on to give a classy acceptance speech, thanking the fans and his fellow creators in the industry. He then got choked up with heartfelt comments about his wife, Kelly, who was in attendance, and about Simon Huck. Jenkins explained, "Simon is more than the co-founder of J&H Comics. He is my dear friend. This award is as much his as it is mine. Without Sy, J&H never would have survived, never mind thrive as we have. Unfortunately, as most of you know, Sy couldn't be here tonight due to his illness. But I know this is being recorded, and he'll see it. So, Sy, thanks for everything you've done for J&H, for the industry, and for both Kelly and me. You are a true ..." Jenkins' voice broke, and he wiped away a tear. He focused on his wife. The small, thin woman with red, frizzy hair was seated at the table right in front of him. Jenkins took a deep breath. "Sy, you are a true superhero. God bless you, my friend. And thank you, everyone. This means a great deal to Kelly and me."

The reaction to Jenkins' acceptance speech was nearly unanimous, as almost everyone in the front tables joined the fans in a standing ovation.

Afterward, as the room was emptying out, Stephen and Zack bumped into a friend. Jed Raft was a fellow Lutheran pastor and a massive man whose cheeks hung down to hide his neck, and his arms seemed to rest on his torso with elbows sticking out. In lieu of his clergy attire, Jed wore a gray suit with a white shirt and a tie sporting Green Lantern. Grant and Charmichael had not seen Raft in some time, so the three men sat back down at one of the tables to catch up. Church matters quickly took a back seat to Zack and Jed comparing thoughts on the awards. Stephen saw that Jed shared Zack's appreciation for Wes Jenkins.

Eventually, the three had to leave the room as staff were starting to break down tables. Upon exiting the arena, Jed noted that he was parked on the other side of the building from where Stephen's Tahoe was.

After shaking hands, Pastor Raft, with a big smile, declared, "Hey, I'll see you guys tomorrow."

Stephen said, "Sounds good," with Zack adding, "Great!"

Stephen and Zack had taken just a few steps in the direction of the parking lot when the door of a VIP entrance opened, and out stepped Wes and Kelly Jenkins, along with another man.

Stephen noticed the group first, and tapped Zack on the upper arm. Zack looked over at the three, and then with large eyes turned back to Stephen. Charmichael hesitated, while the three started walking away. He then said to Stephen, "Let's introduce ourselves."

Grant smiled, and said, "Lead on."

Once they caught up, Zack said, "Excuse me. I hope you don't mind us interrupting?"

The three turned, and Wes Jenkins said, "Of course not..." He then spotted the collars on Charmichael and Grant, and smiled. "Ah, the two pastors in the audience, or is it priests?"

Zack's smile widened. "You have it right. We're pastors at a nearby Lutheran church. I'm Pastor Zack Charmichael and this is Pastor Stephen Grant."

"Did you say Lutheran?" replied Wes, as he shook each man's hand.

"Yes," answered Zack.

Wes said, "This is my wife, Kelly. We're actually Lutherans, of the Missouri Synod variety."

"As are we," provided Grant.

Kelly said, "It's so nice to meet both of you. Whenever this happens, I feel like we're meeting members of our extended family."

Stephen responded, "I'm like that, too, Mrs. Jenkins."

"Oh, please, it's Kelly."

Wes added, "And I've been rude in failing to introduce Brendan Best. He runs this and other conventions, making him our host for the weekend."

Further greetings were followed by Zack seizing the opportunity to talk directly to Jenkins. "I just wanted to say that you're a wonderful writer and artist. Your storytelling is insightful and entertaining. And quite frankly, you're a key reason why I've continued to read and enjoy comic books."

Grant could see the humility and appreciation in Jenkins' response. Jenkins said, "Well, Pastor, thank you so much."

Best interrupted, "Would you all mind if we walked toward my van? I'm supposed to be driving Kelly and Wes to their hotel." He pointed in the same direction where Zack and Stephen were heading.

Zack replied, "I'm sorry if we held you up."

Stephen noted that the van Best pointed to was only a few parking spaces away from the Tahoe.

Wes said, "Not at all. It's a joy for me to meet a couple of pastors who are interested in comic books."

Stephen volunteered, "Zack is the longtime fan. He has been introducing me gradually over the last few years. So far, I've only been able to read collections of *Justice Society of America, Captain America, Nick Fury and S.H.I.E.L.D.* and *Batman*."

"That's certainly a good group for introducing a reader."

Zack added, "Stephen has a certain affinity for spies, detectives and patriotism."

Stephen said, "Zack is right, and I've grown to appreciate good storytelling no matter its form. What would you suggest I read from your body of work?"

Wes answered, "I guess I would suggest *Team 17* or *Agent Cold*."

Zack nodded in agreement.

Stephen said, "I look forward to reading both."

As they approached the van, Wes asked, "Will you two be here tomorrow?"

While Stephen nodded, Zack offered an enthusiastic, "Definitely."

"Come by our table, and I'll have signed omnibuses for each of you."

Zack said, "Wow! That's very kind. Thank you."

Stephen started to respond. "Yes, thank..." But his attention was diverted by what he called a "red alert." During his time as a SEAL and with the CIA, Grant had a knack for knowing when danger loomed, as he would feel a tightness in his ears and head. He noticed that while a few vehicles were still exiting through the parking lot gate, one dark blue sedan actually was pulling into the lot. The car then turned and headed in their direction.

Zack asked, "Stephen?"

No one else in the group was paying attention to the car, with Best nonchalantly using the key remote to unlock the van. At the beep and click of the locks, Stephen stepped forward and said, "Everyone needs to get in the van, please, quickly." He reached forward and slid open the side door of the van.

Zack again queried, "Stephen?"

"No time." He nearly lifted Wes and Kelly Jenkins, each by an arm, into the van. He shoved Best into the open driver's door.

The engine revved higher in the approaching car.

Stephen turned to see Zack standing unmoving, and completely bewildered. Grant grabbed his friend, and tossed him into the van on top of the couple they just met. He yelled, "Stay down!" and shut the van door.

Grant then turned to see the barrels of two shotguns – one sticking through the open window of the sedan's front passenger side door and the other through the back-door window on the same side. As one of the guns was fired, Grant dropped to the ground. The buckshot sprayed the back of the van, far enough away from the four people inside. Grant watched as the barrels of both guns were pulled back into the car. The sedan then started to make a U-turn.

No way.

Grant jumped to his feet, and sprinted to the Tahoe. By the time he was behind the wheel and had the engine started, the sedan was passing through the gates of the parking lot.

Grant saw that the sedan would have to make a right and drive along the other side of the parking lot fence in order to make the escape. He hit the accelerator, and drove toward a gate at the other end of the lot that, if it were not locked, would open onto the road that the sedan was now driving down.

It became a simple race – the sedan speeding along the fence, and Grant urging his Tahoe forward in the hopes of breaking through the gate in time to cut off the escape of the assailants.

The result of this contest was becoming clear to Grant as he calculated the speed of the two vehicles and the converging angle.

Jen's not going to like me wrecking another car. Due to previous encounters with unsavory types, Stephen had wrecked Jennifer's Thunderbird, followed later by Stephen's first Tahoe. *The only real question: Will the Tahoe make it through the fence? Lord, I need your help.*

Grant's Tahoe engaged the chain links at 70 mph. The gate offered no resistance, as the SUV followed Grant's commands and continued to accelerate. Interestingly, the sedan didn't offer all that much resistance either when the Tahoe struck it at high speed.

The front grill of the SUV crashed into the passenger side front panel of the sedan. The much smaller car then spun, slamming into and ricocheting off of the Tahoe's driver's side. The whiplash effect sent the sedan partially flying and sliding. While the Tahoe came to a screeching halt, the sedan hit a short cement barrier running along the far side of the road, jumped over the barrier, and then tumbled down a small embankment.

Grant managed to open his door and slide out from the deployed airbag. At first, he was staggering. But then he gained his balance, and rushed to the spot where the vehicle had disappeared. He jumped over the cement wall, and slid down the hill toward the car, which had come to rest on its roof.

No fire hopefully.

He knelt down, looked inside, and was amazed to see three men moving ever so slightly and moaning in pain.

They survived.

Grant spotted one of the shotguns, and tossed it aside. He then proceeded to pull each man out of the wreck.

Each in his early twenties. Actually looks like pretty minor injuries.

As Stephen dragged the last one away from the car, Zack called down. "Stephen, are you okay?"

"Yes. Have you called 911?"

"I was just about to."

"I'll make the call."

"Okay. What can I do?"

Grant picked up the shotgun, made sure a round was in the chamber, and held the weapon on the three men lying on the ground. "I've got these three covered. Just make sure everyone is alright up there."

"They are. We are." Zack went silent for a few seconds, and then asked, "What the hell just happened?"

"To be honest, I'm not totally sure." He pulled out his smartphone, calling the FBI first and then 911.

Chapter 5

Stephen finished telling the story of the night's events. "Fortunately, my call to Trent meant an FBI team quickly arrived on the scene – which is actually pretty amazing when you think about it." Stephen had worked and become friends with FBI Special Agent Trent Nguyen.

Jennifer was lying next to Stephen in bed. "I'm shocked whenever government – even law enforcement – acts efficiently."

"And you say I'm cynical when it comes to government."

"I speak with the authority of an economist."

"And I offer the real-life anecdotes and experiences."

"Hence, we're such a good team."

Stephen smiled, and continued, "They took away the three assailants, cordoned off the area and cleaned everything up."

"Why did you call the FBI initially?"

"It was a gut call based on a couple of things. I recently read about growing concerns inside of various law enforcement agencies that political disputes on campuses and elsewhere could take more violent turns. And then there was the rundown that Zack gave me on some of the more intolerant impulses among SJW types tied to comic books. As it turned out, Trent confirmed that the FBI is worried about the possibility of the most extreme SJW groups resorting to violent, even deadly, measures."

"Great. Another group to worry about."

"We'll be fine."

She leaned over and kissed him. “I know.”

He added, “I almost forgot to mention that Brendan Best said Zack and I should stop at the VIP window in the morning. We’ll have full access to the entire event for the weekend, even behind the scenes.”

“Zack must be pleased.”

“He is, not to mention that he seemed to be caught between being shocked and exhilarated by everything that happened.”

“I’ve said it before. He looks up to you, including being fascinated by your background. And now he’s seen you in action, so to speak.” She paused, and then asked, “What about Mr. and Mrs. Jenkins?”

“She clearly was shaken. As for Wes, I think the storyteller in him had some appreciation for what unfolded.”

Jennifer looked into his eyes. “You manage to even find action and adventure at a comic con. Although, maybe it’s more fitting there in some sense.”

Stephen shrugged. “One other thing.”

“What’s that?”

“Kelly and Wes are Lutherans.”

“The Lutheran world is small.”

Stephen nodded. “It is.”

After a few minutes of silence, Jennifer observed, “This makes three cars you’ve wrecked.”

Stephen replied, “Unfortunately.”

She smiled and said, “And you wonder why I don’t let you drive the Jeep.”

Chapter 6

"The main thing is that you're both okay," commented Drake Werth, though not exactly in a heartfelt tone.

Werth was seated at a table in the hotel restaurant with Kelly and Wes Jenkins early on Saturday morning. They hadn't provided much in terms of details – at the request of the FBI and Pastor Stephen Grant – on what occurred the previous night. They merely said that Brendan Best and the two of them had been saved from an attack after the awards dinner. The couple managed to deflect most of Werth's questions.

Kelly replied, "Thanks, Drake."

Drake looked at Wes. "Do you still want to go over what we had talked about?"

Wes swallowed the last bite of his omelet, and said, "Yes. We need to get things clear."

Kelly looked uncomfortable.

Werth said, "We have to make some changes. We need to bring our stories and themes more in line with what much of the industry is doing."

Wes replied, "Meaning that you want to toss aside our long history and success at J&H, and replace it with a political agenda."

"It's not a political agenda. It's just dealing with the changes in the marketplace. You might not like it, but this is the reality."

"What reality is that, Drake? I don't see a great influx of sales and success resulting from this shift among a few key industry players. If anything, their numbers have suffered. I think this rather dramatic tonal shift has occurred due to immature selfishness, inexperience and arrogance among too many creators and publishers. They're not responding to their market; instead, they're ignoring their audience and fans."

Drake took a deep breath. "Sy sold me his share in this business. This is going to happen, Wes, and you need to get onboard."

"Or what?"

"Or..." Drake hesitated and glanced at Kelly. But then he continued. "Well, let's not think that way."

Wes leaned forward. "Yes, Drake, let's take a moment and think that way. We own this business together, you and I, 50-50. We need to be honest. Or what?"

"Look, Wes, we can't afford to look like we're bigoted and behind the times."

"Drake, did you just call me a bigot?"

"No, I don't want us to appear..."

"So, let me get this straight. If I don't agree to politicize my stories and characters with left-wing bias, then I'm a bigot? Is that what you're saying?"

"That's how it will be perceived. That article you wrote in *The Wall Street Journal...*"

"Yes?"

"That was..." Drake hesitated, and then completed his thought. "That wasn't helpful. It put us at odds with so many people in the industry and new readers."

"Drake, if Sy or I cared about what people in the industry thought, then we never would have started J&H. But I am very much concerned about readers. And Drake, I think that J&H has kept readers front and center. Too much of the rest of the industry has abandoned the fans, again, for an agenda, because their biases and politics don't allow them to see or even consider other views."

"That's bullshit, Wes. You just don't understand."

Wes took a deep breath. Anger faded from his face, replaced by a kind of calm. It was reflected in the tone of his voice. “This has been a productive meeting.”

Drake’s voice made his annoyance clear. “Productive? How do you figure that?”

“We’ve cleared away the clouds. We know where each person stands, and we can make decisions accordingly.”

“There’s only one decision possible, Wes. Either you’re going to move ahead with a new path for J&H or you’ll be left behind.”

Wes actually smiled at that comment. He reached in his pocket, pulled out cash in a money clip, and peeled off a few bills. He dropped them on the table. “That should cover breakfast. Kelly and I have to get to the arena. I like to arrive early, and make sure we’re ready for people who come by the table.”

Kelly and Wes rose from their chairs. Drake looked up with fury etched on his face.

Kelly didn’t bother to say anything to Drake. Instead, she started walking away from the table.

Wes, however, lingered, and said, “Take care, Drake.”

The irritated Werth replied, “Yes, yes, of course. We’ll talk more later.”

Wes simply said, “Perhaps.” He then turned to catch up with his wife.

Kelly whispered, “You were far kinder than I would have been. It took all my strength to refrain from calling him a jackass.”

Chapter 7

With Stephen's Tahoe on life support, Zack drove to the Suffolk Arena on Saturday morning. After passing through arena security, they picked up the special VIP passes left by Brendan Best. Now, they had the run of the entire building.

A wide concourse sported large windows on the outside, and a mix of concession stands and doors into the main arena around the inside. For this event, the concourse was called the "Creators' Circle," with table after table featuring assorted artists and writers, as well as some actors who portrayed various superhero, sci-fi and fantasy characters in movies, television shows and video games.

Stephen, of course, knew about people dressing up as their favorite characters at these events, but this being the first time he was witnessing cosplay, he couldn't help but stare.

Jen guessed that I might experience a little culture shock.

But since the point was to engage with others, no one minded his looking. To the contrary, they enjoyed it.

Given that they would be leaving the arena directly for St. Mary's Saturday evening Divine Service, Stephen and Zack once again came in clergy attire. The only accompaniment was Zack's backpack with assorted books he wanted signed by writers and artists.

Inside the main section of the arena where fans usually watched minor league hockey, indoor soccer and college basketball, two-thirds of the floor had rows of vendors selling anything a fan of comics, movies, video games, and

TV shows might desire. A massive curtain hung from the rafters, sectioning off a stage upon which assorted stars – from broad down to very niche markets – would be speaking and answering questions over the coming two days.

As they walked, a few people called out to Stephen and Zack with comments like, "Hey, *Preacher*, right?"

Grant and Charmichael smiled in response the first couple of times. Stephen then gave Zack a quizzical look. Zack provided a quick rundown of the comic book character Preacher, also noting that it had made the leap to a television show.

Stephen queried, "Any good?"

Zack indifferently shrugged, and said, "Lousy theology."

Their first stop was at the J&H Comics tables, and they were greeted warmly by Wes and Kelly Jenkins.

Wes told them, "Please come around," indicating that the two pastors should move behind the tables. After following Wes' request, the four spoke in low voices about the previous night's events. But as a line of fans started to form, Wes said, "Okay, as promised…" He reached down and picked up a massive, oversized, 1,000-page-plus book, and placed it on the table, followed by another of similar size. He opened and signed each book. Wes then handed the *Team 17* tome to Zack and *Agent Cold* to Stephen.

Stephen said, "Thanks very much. Are you sure we don't owe you anything?"

Wes replied, "Oh, please, no. Considering what we owe you after last night."

Kelly prompted, "Wes, the line."

He looked over, and said, "Right." He turned back, and said to Zack, "I assume you guys are going to explore the rest of the convention?"

"Yes."

"Then leave these heavy books here, and go enjoy yourselves."

"Thanks, Wes, we appreciate it," said Zack.

Wes took the books back, and placed them in a box. "Just let Kelly or me know when you want them back."

He then walked over and said to his fans. "Sorry about the small delay. Thanks, everybody, for coming. I'm happy to sign whatever you brought, and as you can see, we have pretty much the full line of J&H books available for purchase, and at special convention prices."

Approvals emanated from the growing line.

Watching Jenkins start signing, Zack said to Stephen, "He's a good guy."

Stephen agreed. "He is."

"As for the next step, I was planning to grab some signatures while early lines are still short. Do you want to go with me, or explore a bit on your own?"

As if on cue, Grant's smartphone rumbled in his jacket pocket. "Hold that thought." He pulled out the phone, and saw that the call was from the FBI's Trent Nguyen. He looked at Zack, "I have to take this call. You go, and I'll catch up."

Zack said, "Sounds good."

As Zack moved away, Grant answered the call. "Trent?"

"Yes, Stephen. How are you after last night?"

Grant moved away from the stream of people to a spot along the windows with no one in earshot. "I'm fine. What's the deal with the three attackers?"

"To put it gently, these guys have problems. It didn't take too long for our people to find their online rants."

"What were those about?"

"They billed themselves as the Trinity for Social Justice."

"How original."

"Yeah, right. They wrote out their delusions or intentions in story form – long, rambling and often-crossing-the-border-into-incoherent screeds. The basic gist is that three warriors serve up a violent brand of justice on a pretty lengthy list of people the militant Left would dislike, including the military, cops, conservative commentators and politicians, and priests and pastors – sorry about that."

"Hey, I'm honored."

Nguyen continued, "The list goes on, but it also includes a rant about killing assorted men involved in starting the comic book industry, but who are deemed unworthy due to their, and I'm quoting here, 'exercising patriarchal and white privilege.' If you read that particular piece, it unfortunately lines up with what these three tried to do."

Grant shook his head while listening. "A combination of hatred, ignorance, twisted ideology, and detachment from reality."

"You nailed it." Nguyen added, "There's way too much of that combination going around these days."

"What's next?"

"We've got a few more people to follow up with, and then we'll be making an announcement on the arrests probably on Monday or Tuesday. I'll do the best I can to keep your name out of the media."

"I appreciate that, and thanks for the call."

"Thanks for what you did. This is the least I could do." Nguyen then asked, "Do you mind if I ask you for a couple of favors?"

"Not at all."

"You're at this convention today and tomorrow?"

"That's the plan."

Nguyen paused, and then queried, "Without interfering with what you and Pastor Charmichael are doing, can you just watch for any further potential problems? Anyone that… Well, you know."

"No problem, Trent. I'll let you know if anything that really matters catches my attention. What's the second favor?"

"That's a personal one. I've kind of embraced this Captain America thing." Trent Nguyen not only ranked as one of the most decorated agents in FBI history, but his parents, an American nurse stationed in South Vietnam during the war and a Vietnamese businessman, taught him from a very young age to appreciate the United States. His patriotism and willingness to stop evildoers earned him the nickname of "Captain America" among colleagues at the FBI. "I'm looking for an *Avengers #4* from 1964. It's the return of Captain America."

Comic fans where you might least expect them.

Nguyen continued, "When I was growing up, comic books played a big part in getting me interested in reading, and I guess not so ironically, my favorite was Captain America. Funny, I never told anyone at the Bureau that, but here I am telling you."

"I get that a lot with the collar."

"Hmmm. I bet. Well, would you mind?"

Grant replied, "Not a problem. Zack and I will be happy to keep an eye out."

Nguyen warned, "I'm looking for one that's in decent condition that I can frame. It's going to be very pricey, though, and I'll obviously reimburse you, but if you don't want to do it, I completely understand."

"I'm more than happy to do it, and I think Zack will actually be ecstatic."

"Thanks. I appreciate it," replied Nguyen.

After the call, Stephen decided to leave Zack to his pursuit for signatures, for now, and explore the event on his own, doing a little people watching as he did.

As he strolled, Grant observed attendees, from pre-teens to some in their seventies, enjoying a shared interest with varying intensity. Some came simply to meet favorite creators or in pursuit of certain publications. For others, it was an excuse to do something with family or a group of friends – more about social engagement than appreciating certain stories via page or screen.

There were others for whom it was all of the above, including being dressed in full character regalia. One couple in this category not only caught Grant's eye, but drew the attention of seemingly everyone else as they strode through the event. It was evident that the two spent considerable time in the gym. The man stood at six foot four and the woman at just over six feet. He was dressed as Hawkman, with the costume showing off his muscular arms and much of his rock-hard torso. He was wearing a hawk mask and had large wings coming out of his back. He also brandished a Thanagarian Mace. Meanwhile, the woman's blue eyes, long black hair, thin waist and strong arms and legs seemed to make her a natural Wonder Woman, with the bathing-suit-sized costume of red, gold and blue, with white stars, a natural fit. The golden lasso hanging on the side of the costume, silver bracelets, and high red boots completed the look perfectly.

Grant watched as fellow fans were attracted to the couple, asking to pose with them for pictures.

And since they're superheroes, they're more than happy to do that for these fine citizens. Grant smiled at his private joke. *Jen would have rolled her eyes at that one.*

Finally, while a tiny minority, Grant did spot a few individuals here and there who probably didn't have much else in life, and had perhaps immersed themselves too deeply in fantasy. Of course, this was not a phenomenon unique to this venue. As a pastor and during his CIA days, Grant had met such people before; they simply had different interests or work into which they would get lost. It was not unusual, thankfully, for Grant to also witness someone eventually entering and bringing balance to the lives of such people. That included, during his time as a pastor, frequently witnessing the Lord using someone to help bring the light of Christ and His Church into such individuals' lives.

Grant was snapped out of his musings by someone saying, "Excuse me, Father?"

Stephen realized it was Hawkman. "Yes. Sorry, I was lost in thought." He reflected on how surreal this was as he was talking to two people who looked like they could play the parts of Hawkman and Wonder Woman in a movie. "I'm Pastor Stephen Grant." As he shook each person's hand, Grant continued, "And you are Hawkman and Wonder Woman."

As the two smiled in response, Grant judged that they were both in their early thirties.

The man said, "In addition to being Hawkman, I'm Guy Nodell, and Wonder Woman is my wife, Diane."

Stephen raised an eyebrow, and said, "Diane? Not Diana?"

Diane said, "Close, I know. It's nice to meet you. Guy and I knew you weren't just portraying Preacher or the pastor from *Man of Steel.*"

Stephen caught the reference from the Superman movie. "No, I'm the real deal; a pastor at St. Mary's Lutheran Church in Manorville. I'm here with our other pastor as well. You two seem to be quite the hit with fellow fans."

They both smiled broadly. Guy said, "Yeah, it's kind of cool, and a change of pace for us."

Stephen asked, "And what do you do when not battling evildoers?"

"We restore and repair classic cars."

"That's interesting. How did that come about, if you don't mind me asking?"

Diane said, "We met in the Army. We were both mechanics. If it ran on wheels or tracks, we maintained and fixed them. After our tours were up, we got married, and not long after went into business for ourselves."

"Nice. Congratulations."

The couple replied in unison, "Thanks."

"I was a SEAL, but I won't hold the Army thing against you."

They went on to share some good-natured Navy-Army ribbing. When Zack approached the group, Stephen introduced the couple to his friend.

Diane eventually asked, "How about a quick photo?"

Stephen replied, "You're asking to take a photo with us?"

She nodded. "That's why Guy and I came over in the first place. Meeting a pastor at a con is pretty rare, never mind two."

A fan in his late teens wearing a Justice League shirt became entranced when Wonder Woman handed him a smartphone and asked if he would take the group's picture. He dutifully snapped several shots with her phone and then with Zack's. After Diane then took a picture with him, the fan, with flushed face, thanked her several times.

Zack asked Guy, "Can I check out your mace?"

"Sure." He handed over the golden weapon.

Zack smiled. "Wow, it's actually heavier than I thought it would be."

"I made it myself – carved it out of an oak block, painted it and applied a protective coating."

As he handed the mace back, Zack commented, "Nice work."

"Thanks." Guy then pulled business cards out of a back pocket, and handed one each to Zack and Stephen. He added, "By the way, if you have any car needs, let us know."

Grant said, "Thanks. Actually, I probably will since I just wrecked my SUV."

Chapter 8

Stephen and Zack's VIP tickets not only got them into a lunch mainly reserved for the event's various speakers, but also seats in front of the stage.

Taking the two seats on the stage were Wes Jenkins and Brendan Best. The portion of the arena's seating set aside for speakers and panels was filled, and after being officially introduced by Best, Jenkins received a rousing ovation.

Sitting in two director-style chairs, with a table in between them where water bottles rested, the two men were relaxed, having an enjoyable conversation about Jenkins' career in the industry that they were both part of and clearly loved. When the two touched on various characters created by Jenkins, parts of the crowd would shout out their approval.

As their discussion approached the end of its allotted time, Best asked, "So, what's next?"

There was a notable pause by Jenkins, and the room went quiet. He looked out at the audience, and then back to Best. "Actually, Brendan, it looks like there are going to be some big changes coming."

Jenkins' tone led to some murmuring in the crowd. Best pressed, "What changes, Wes? I hope they're positive."

"So do I." He took a deep breath, and then smiled. "Actually, I'm excited about it."

Best smiled as well, looked out at the audience, and then back to Jenkins. "It will be just between us, and I promise not to tell." That generated laughs. "Please, what's happening?"

"As some of you might know, I wrote a piece in *The Wall Street Journal* recently about the comic book business."

Scattered boos were quickly overwhelmed by clapping and a few cheers.

Jenkins looked out at the audience, and said, "That reaction basically reflects the reaction I've received overall."

Best interjected, "And we have a panel specifically addressing your article tomorrow."

Jenkins responded, "Right, so this is not the time to crawl inside that topic. But my decision is at least partially rooted in those issues. It breaks my heart, but I'm leaving J&H."

Amidst the buzz of the crowd, shouts of "No!" and "Please, no!" could be heard.

Best asked, "Why?"

"I need to make sure that the characters I create stay true to who they are, and my work can maintain what I think is best about comics. So, I am starting my own publishing house."

Applause and cheers erupted.

Best waited for the sound to die down a bit, and then persisted, "But what about your life's work? Won't you be leaving all of those characters behind?"

The room again went silent.

Jenkins smiled. "Unlike many of my co-creators, I own the copyright to all of my characters. When we set up J&H, Sy insisted that I actually own the characters. We trusted each other, of course, but Sy understood that a day might come when, for whatever reason, J&H might have to come to an end or change in a big way. That time actually has come. So, J&H basically has had the exclusive deal to publish my works, until I decide to end that agreement. I'm going to do that, and then *Agent Cold*, *Undisclosed*, *Team 17* and everyone else will be coming with me for new adventures."

But for the few who booed earlier, each person in the audience rose to their feet. They clapped, with many serving up hoots of approval. Both Zack and Stephen were standing and applauding, with Zack being particularly pleased.

Chapter 9

After Wes Jenkins dropped his bombshell on the comic book community, next came the panel that Stephen was looking forward to the most. His inner film buff came to life with a discussion among three directors and two producers of various Marvel films.

After enjoying the wide-ranging discussion of filmmaking, Stephen then found out that his VIP pass meant that he was able to join the movie makers for an exclusive informal chat and photos.

Zack dutifully took pictures of Stephen with the group.

Okay, I guess this is my nerd moment of the weekend.

Stephen then did the same in return for Zack.

It also became clear to Stephen that he and Zack received a bit more time with the filmmakers due to the collars. The three directors in particular seemed interested, amused or both by having pastors in attendance at a con, not to mention donning VIP badges.

Eventually, Zack was the one who had to remind Stephen that they needed to leave in order to get ready for the Saturday evening Divine Service at St. Mary's. Stephen looked at his watch, and with a hint of disappointment, said, "Oh, yeah, right."

As good-byes were said, Stephen decided to give each filmmaker his card. He said to the group, "Feel free to stop by St. Mary's." He read the responses as two being indifferent, one being courteous, and two seemingly appreciative of the invitation.

After making their way back onto the main concourse, Zack led the way to the J&H Comics tables. The line was far longer than earlier in the day, and there was Wes signing, laughing and posing for pictures with fans.

Kelly Jenkins spotted and once again called Zack and Stephen behind the tables. She had placed the two omnibuses signed by Wes in a bag with a sturdy handle. "I assume you two have to get to church."

Zack said, "We do. Please thank Wes, again. I don't want to disturb him with that line. We'll make sure to see you guys tomorrow."

"Do you mind if we come to church at St. Mary's in the morning?"

"Mind?" replied Zack. "Of course not. That would be wonderful."

Stephen thought Zack might explode.

Kelly continued, "Thanks. Your early service works perfectly for us in order to get here on time."

Zack smiled. "We'll see you both in the morning."

Kelly hugged each man, and then went back to helping her husband.

As the two started to leave, Stephen almost bumped into two new arrivals behind the J&H tables. He said, "Hello."

A man and a woman were shifting books onto one of the J&H tables that was not being used. As they shook hands, Stephen introduced himself and Zack.

The two were in their mid-twenties. The man – slightly overweight, black hair, and dark complexion – said, "Hi, I'm Diego Delarosa."

The woman was tiny – less than five feet tall – and she had a round face, large brown eyes, and dark brown hair. She offered, "Hello, I'm Tara Tower."

Zack blurted out, "You two are a great team."

They both smiled, and thanked him. Zack explained to Stephen that Tara wrote, and Diego drew, colored and penciled for J&H Comics. Grant nodded in response.

Zack continued, “I appreciate new voices that get the history of the genre, but bring innovative and creative ideas to their work – as you two do.”

Diego pointed toward Wes, and replied, “We’ve been fortunate to learn from the best.”

Zack said, “That must be a great experience.”

Tara replied, “It has been.”

“Forgive me if I shouldn’t ask,” interjected Stephen, “but will you two be going with Wes to his new venture?”

Diego and Tara glanced at each other, and then she responded, “Well, we hope so.”

Diego added, “This is very new, so we’re not sure what’s going to happen.”

“I see,” said Stephen. “I’ll keep you both in my prayers.”

The two creators hesitated, but then offered their thanks.

Chapter 10

Kelly and Wes Jenkins lingered just a bit after the early Divine Service on Sunday morning at St. Mary's Lutheran Church. They wound up, as a result, at the end of the line heading out of the nave.

Kelly shook Zack's hand, and said, "That was a wonderful service. Thank you so much."

Zack seemed a bit taken off guard. "Oh, you're welcome."

She continued, "You have to understand that when Wes and I travel, getting to church can be hard. And then when we do, the services, on occasion, wander from the liturgy."

Zack nodded. "Ah, I understand."

Stephen invited, "Whenever you're on the east end of Long Island, make sure you visit us at St. Mary's."

Kelly smiled, and Wes said, "We most certainly will."

Stephen asked, "By the way, where is home for you two?"

Kelly answered, "We live just outside of Austin, Texas."

Stephen replied, "Nice city."

"We like it," she replied.

Wes added, "I love the creative community there. It's vibrant."

Zack said, "I assume that's where the new company will set up shop?"

Wes said, "Yes. I have a studio in the city, and there's an opportunity to expand that space. I've been thinking about this, but nothing was definite until I spoke with Drake yesterday morning."

"Drake?" asked Stephen.

"Drake Werth purchased Sy's share of J&H Comics."

Both Zack and Stephen nodded slightly in response.

Wes continued, "With his illness, Sy had to sell his part of the business. And Sy and I agreed on Drake as the buyer. We thought he had a full appreciation for what we had accomplished, and for our vision and mission for the company."

This is still hard on him.

Kelly patted her husband on the shoulder.

Wes added, "But things quickly changed when the purchase was complete. It turns out that Drake wants to go the political route – the exact path I criticized in my *Journal* piece."

Zack said, "I'm sorry to hear that."

Stephen commented, "That must be extremely frustrating."

Wes then shrugged and actually smiled. "At first, it was. I thought I'd have to spend years battling Drake. But then I decided that would be a horrible, draining experience. So, instead, I have an out. I own the characters that I created. I'm starting a new company, and Drake can do what he wants with J&H Comics. I'll lose some money whether he or one of his people buys me out. But the real value ends up being in the characters and the talent. And when I say talent, by the way, that very much includes Kelly. In terms of directing the entire process of going from creators to the market, that's all been Kelly at J&H."

Stephen replied, "That's a great attitude, and it sounds like it should work out." He then shifted gears slightly. "Zack and I met Tara and Diego yesterday."

Kelly said, "I just love the two of them. They're like sponges around Wes, looking to soak up everything he can teach, and they're very talented. But best of all, they're just good people."

Zack looked at Wes, and asked, "Are they going to go with you to the new firm?"

"I certainly hope so. I'm planning to offer them both jobs this morning."

Zack said, "From what I saw, they'll jump at the opportunity."

"I hope so. The only problem is that J&H actually owns the characters they've created. So, if they come with me, they'll lose control over those creations."

Zack replied, "I see."

"But, at the same time, I plan on giving them an opportunity to create new characters, and give them the same copyright ownership that I have had with J&H."

Stephen interjected, "I'm pretty sure that Tara and Diego will be going with you."

Kelly added, "I think you've read it right, Pastor."

After having finished helping the altar guild, Jennifer came down the center aisle of the nave. As she approached the group, Stephen introduced her to Kelly and Wes.

Jennifer said, "It's so great to meet both of you." After exchanging niceties, Jennifer said to Wes, "My husband tells me that you're an excellent storyteller."

"That's very kind." He lowered his voice. "And he's quite the pastor, not only in leading a church service but in capturing assailants. It's rather unusual."

Jennifer smirked and said, "Yes, I hear that more often than one might think."

Wes added, "And I know your work as well, Dr. Grant. I've read some of your op-eds in recent years, and I enjoyed your book."

Jennifer graciously replied, "Thank you very much."

Kelly said, "I hope we can continue this conversation at another time, but right now, we have to get to the arena."

Chapter 11

After an impromptu meeting delayed their departure from St. Mary's, Stephen could see that Zack was anxious to leave immediately for the final day of the convention. So, off they went in clergy attire, once again, for a few more hours of comics, sci-fi, fantasy and more.

Just over a half-hour later, Zack and Stephen approached the J&H Comics tables. While he was dutifully signing for and taking photos with fans, Wes' eyes and attention were being diverted to a less-than-quiet conversation happening behind him.

Drake Werth was speaking to Tara Tower and Diego Delarosa. He had an intense look on his face. As Stephen and Zack arrived at the tables, Stephen could hear the anger in Werth's voice.

Drake said, "So, you're just going to walk away from the characters that you created?"

Tara answered, "We're going to have to do that. We don't really have a choice."

Werth lowered his voice, trying to sound more reassuring. "But you do. Stay with J&H, and you'll both continue writing those characters, while creating more."

Diego said, "I regret losing control over those characters, but we've made our decision."

His soothing tone once again evaporated, and while pointing a finger, Werth declared, "That's a stupid decision. The two of you will fail without the name of J&H Comics."

Tara unleashed her annoyance. "I think you know that's a load of garbage, Drake. People care and love J&H Comics because of who is behind the name. That's no longer going to be the case, and you're aggravated because, deep down in, you know that. You're desperate."

While Tara was speaking, Diego started nodding in support.

Drake replied, "You little shits."

Kelly, who had been lingering near the conversation, stepped in, and said, "Drake, please. What are you doing?"

Werth turned on her. "Shut up, Kelly. You're going to see."

Wes jumped up from the chair, and took several strides toward Werth and the others. Meanwhile, Zack and Stephen weren't the only ones watching this conflict play out, as it drew the attention of a long line of fans.

Wes stopped a mere two feet in front of Werth, and said, "Drake, don't ever speak to my wife that way again. You can apologize, calm down and act like an adult, or you can leave."

Stephen saw Werth clench his fists. Grant was ready to spring forward, if necessary.

Werth gradually unclenched his hands, and took a deep breath. His eyes scanned the four people standing in front of him. Then he stopped to look at Wes. He leaned in, and whispered, "I'm not going to let you get away with this, you son of a bitch."

Wes simply shook his head in response. He then turned and said to his wife, "Are you okay, Kelly?"

She nodded.

Wes gave her a quick hug, and then said to the three, "Hey, take whatever time you need, of course, and then let's get back to the fans." Wes walked back to the place where he had been signing books, and said to those waiting, "Sorry about that, friends. But even the comic book business can get a little testy. But we're back on track, so let's sign some books and take some selfies. Sound good?"

The group in line applauded.

As Tara and Diego moved to return to the table where they had been signing books earlier, Diego put his arm around Tara's shoulder, and whispered, "Wow, you were great."

She responded, "Thanks. I thought I was going to puke."

Once they sat down, fans began to wander up.

Werth had turned to look out the large windows at the parking lot, with his arms folded.

Stephen could see that Kelly was still bothered, however, as she moved about nervously. He looked at Zack, and said, "Come on."

The two pastors moved behind the tables, passing Werth and reaching Kelly. Stephen said, "Hey, Kelly, are you alright?"

She had been looking down and didn't see the two men approaching, so she reacted with a small jump. "Oh, hello. Yes, I guess I'm okay. Thanks."

Zack pressed, "Are you sure?"

Kelly took a deep breath. "Yes, I am. I just don't like this entire mess. I mean, I agree with Wes. He's a good man, and wouldn't do this if I disagreed. It's just that when things like that happen, it's very stressful."

Zack reassured, "I understand. It can't be easy."

"It's not. But it is the right thing to do." She paused, and glanced over the shoulders of Stephen and Zack at Drake not that far away. "I'm going to avoid this afternoon's panel."

Zack asked, "Which one?"

"The one debating the issues that Wes raised in his article. We've been living what Wes described, and now it's hitting hardest. Drake is going to be on that panel as well. I'm just going to stay here and take care of the tables."

Zack smiled, and said, "Well, you'll get some quiet time then, as everyone else will be jammed in to see that panel."

Kelly replied, "Yes, I know, and that's just fine with me."

As Kelly shifted their conversation to how much she enjoyed St. Mary's and asking questions about the church, Werth pulled out his cellphone while walking away from the J&H tables.

Chapter 12

Zack and Stephen settled into their VIP, second-row seats in front of the stage. Diego and Tara were seated next to them. As she'd planned, Kelly remained back at the J&H tables.

Five stools, with a microphone resting on each, awaited the participants for the final panel of the con. At the back of the stage stood a massive screen, which allowed fans in the higher seats to better see the speakers.

As five men walked onto the stage, most of the crowd broke into applause and cheers. At the same time, few took much notice of some 40 people sprinkled throughout the crowd pulling out and putting on red t-shirts.

When the audience quieted down, Brendan Best, who was moderating this group, said, "Thanks for that warm welcome. So, this might be the most highly charged panel of our event as we discuss a controversial article that Wes Jenkins wrote for *The Wall Street Journal* on the state of and challenges faced by the comic book industry – an industry that we all love and have been here the last two days celebrating."

Some hoots, boos and murmurs rippled through the audience.

Best raised a hand and smiled. "Now, I know the comic book, sci-fi and fantasy community. We are an open-minded, respectful bunch. In many ways, we appreciate our diversity and have long been civil in our disagreements."

That generated applause from the crowd and the other four people seated on stage.

Brendan nodded in response. "That's great. Now, we are so lucky to have these creators with us. The *four* truly are *fantastic* as a group, and for this discussion, break into two *dynamic duos* squaring off to discuss and, yes, debate some important issues for the industry." He stopped, looked out at the crowd with a smirk, and said, "See what I did there?" That generated a few chuckles and some good-natured groans. He continued, "Okay, sorry." Brendan proceeded to introduce Wes and fellow comics writer and artist Max Sayers. The two had worked together many times over the years. The other pairing was Drake Werth and Nathan Lieberman, a longtime artist in the business known for the realism in his drawings.

After the introductions, Brendan said, "So, let's start with Wes." Best looked at Jenkins, and said, "If you don't mind, I'd like you to start us off by summing up the points made in your article."

Wes raised the microphone, and started, "Thanks, Brendan. I'd be glad to..."

Jenkins was interrupted when four individuals donning red shirts jumped to their feet and started chanting what was written on their shirts. "Stop White Privilege! Stop Sexism! Stop Hate!"

Some in the crowd shouted, "Sit down" or "Shut up!" or both.

Others booed.

A few applauded, and called out, "Yeah!"

Looking out at the protestors, Wes asked, "Is this really what we're going to do?"

Best said, "There's no reason for this. Let's have the discussion, and then there will be plenty of time for questions."

The four simply continued to scream out their mantra.

Best added, "We'd like everyone to be able to enjoy this panel."

The four continued the shouting.

The boos in response grew louder.

Best shook his head sadly, and looked off stage at his team. Away from the microphone, he said, "I guess we're going to need security."

A few members of the event's security personnel wearing bright yellow shirts moved toward the protestors. When security started to lead those shouting out of their respective rows, four more people in red shirts sprang to their feet elsewhere, and joined in the chant.

Grant looked around the room, counting the number of people he could see wearing the red shirts. He whispered to Zack, "There might be forty of these people. They planned this well. If four of them get to their feet each time the previous four start to be taken out, this is going to last a really long time."

Zack was clearly irritated. "They don't want anyone who possibly disagrees with them to speak."

Stephen nodded. "Like I said on Friday, Stalinists."

Zack looked at those shouting. "Young and angry, and so misinformed. I'm guessing most are in college. Do you think they even know who Stalin was?"

"Probably not. And I'm very confident in saying that most have never heard of Marcuse, even though they unwittingly are influenced by him."

On stage, Max Sayers spoke loudly into his microphone. "What are you people trying to achieve? What are you possibly accomplishing by shouting down a discussion with both sides represented?"

Most of the audience applauded in response.

The eight standing protestors continued their chanting, but another red shirt closer to the stage stood up, and called out, "You're the problem. Stop the privilege."

Sayers laughed, and replied, "That's funny. If you didn't notice, I'm black. What kind of privilege exactly are you talking about?"

The young man who shouted at the stage, who happened to be white, seemed temporarily thrown by Sayers' response.

But then he called back, "You're just part of the system. You just make them feel better."

Sayers lowered his microphone, turned to Jenkins, and whispered, "That little shit."

Wes nodded and shrugged in response.

Werth then spoke to the protestors. "Hey, I'm on your side, but..."

Eight more red shirts jumped to their feet, and yelled back. "Liar!" "Bullshit!"

Off to the left of the stage, a young woman with half of her head shaved and the rest of her hair colored purple caught Werth's attention by shouting, "You're not on my side. You're just another old white guy who doesn't have a clue. How can you speak for me? You should just get out of the way, just die, and let us do what needs to be done."

The shock of being attacked in such a way was evident on Werth's face. He looked at Lieberman, who merely rolled his eyes in response.

More boos reverberated throughout the audience. People shouted back at the protestors. Security personnel didn't know what to do next.

More red shirts stood up and started shouting.

Best's face revealed a growing distress. Jenkins and Sayers wore expressions of exasperation, while the shock on Werth's face merely morphed into confusion. Lieberman seemed a bit amused by it all.

Grant's smartphone rumbled in his pocket. He took it out and saw that the call was from the FBI's Trent Nguyen. He answered, "Trent, hold on for a couple of minutes. I can't hear you."

Stephen said to Zack, "I'm going to find a place where I can hear this call."

Zack nodded, but said, "Good luck with that."

Grant exited the row, and started to climb the stairs. At the top, he spotted Guy and Diane Nodell, once again dressed as Hawkman and Wonder Woman. The two were standing off to the side on a walkway that circled the arena. The couple looked at Stephen and shook their heads in unison at what was transpiring. Grant nodded in response, and then turned toward the doors exiting onto the concourse.

Chapter 13

After pushing the door to the concourse open, Stephen started to raise the smartphone to his ear. But he froze in place when he saw Kelly Jenkins being shoved out a door to his far left. She was surrounded by three men. Grant spotted a gun being held by at least one man.

In the distance, past a stretch of fountains, statues and benches, was the parking lot. A white van sat curbside with its side door open, and a man standing and waiting.

Crap. Armed. At least five counting the driver. I need help.

Grant instinctively said into his phone, "Trent, Kelly Jenkins is being kidnapped. I've got to go."

As he shoved the phone in his pocket, Grant turned and moved back inside the arena. He ran up to Guy and Diane Nodell. "Someone is being taken, and I need your help, now."

The couple didn't hesitate.

Guy replied, "Right."

Diane said, "Okay."

A pastor, a person dressed as Hawkman and a cosplay Wonder Woman running to the arena exit drew some attention, even as the protestors continued to derail the panel.

As the three ran by, a perplexed Pastor Jed Raft asked, "Stephen?"

Grant simply replied, "Jed."

The three exploded through the door onto the concourse. Guy and Diane followed Stephen as he turned left. Grant looked out the large windows, and saw that Kelly and her kidnappers were still a distance from the van. They weren't moving all that quickly, trying not to attract unwarranted attention.

Good.

As the three ran, Grant said, "They're trying to take Wes Jenkins' wife, and they appear to be armed."

Grant wasn't sure what response he expected from this couple that he had met the day before and spoken to just once.

Guy declared, "Not today."

And Diane added, "This will not happen."

Stephen quickly gained a full appreciation for the two.

Grant threw open the door to the outside, and picked up the pace running after the abductors. But he was soon overtaken by Guy on one side and Diane on the other.

The three walking with Kelly had their backs to the unique figures racing toward them. But the kidnapper standing by the van door caught a glimpse of the unusual group. He hesitated for a moment, seemingly trying to digest what he was seeing. He finally called out, "Look out!"

The three holding Kelly looked closer at their companion, but had not yet turned around.

The guard yelled again, "Behind you." He pulled out a gun, but didn't have a clean shot.

Grant called out, "Gun!"

The ground between the three heroes and the villains was quickly being eaten up.

Guy and Diane were now a couple of strides ahead of Grant.

The three kidnappers finally began to turn – from Grant's perspective, one to the right of Kelly, another to the left, and the last behind her. Like the man by the van, the three with Kelly paused at seeing two superheroes and a pastor coming at them.

Grant spotted Diane pulling the golden lasso – actually a formidable whip – off her belt, and continuing at full speed toward the assailant on the right.

At the same time, Guy slowed slightly as he lifted the mace above his head.

The kidnapper to the left already had his gun out, and started to raise it. The other two reached inside their coats for weapons.

Grant calculated that the group of kidnappers was now only a dozen yards away.

Guy finally hurled his wooden mace, and it struck the kidnapper on the left in the chest with considerable force. The man fell backwards, with the gun flying out of his hand.

To the right, as the kidnapper was withdrawing his gun from its holster, Diane aimed and snapped her lasso. The end of the whip struck the side of the man's face. He screamed out a series of obscenities, and reached for the new gash on his cheek. He didn't drop the gun, but that didn't matter. Diane's final stride turned into a leap. She moved through the air, and as she descended, her fist crashed into the gash she had just caused. The kidnapper dropped hard to the cement.

As his two associates fell away, the third man pulled his gun out and tried to grab Kelly by the hair.

Grant screamed an order. "Kelly, get down!"

Kelly Jenkins started to dive to the ground. Grant was pleased with her quick reaction, and he launched his body forward. The kidnapper got off a shot, but it skirted by Grant. His body flew over Kelly's and then crashed into the kidnapper. Grant drove the man to the ground. Stephen heard the air rush out of the man's lungs.

Lying on top of the kidnapper, Grant looked up to see what was happening with the guard standing by the van and the driver inside. As he began to figure out how these last two could be stopped, Grant heard many footsteps coming from behind him, along with assorted shouts and hoots.

More than a dozen comic-con attendees, some in costume but most not, started streaming by Grant. He rose to more of a crouching position on top of the kidnapper, and on each side of him, Diane and Guy had control over the person they took down.

Oh, God, no. Those guys are armed.

He called out, "No, wait, don't!"

But his pleas were drowned out or ignored.

Grant watched as the guard outside the van started to panic. He put his gun away, and scrambled to shut the van's side door. He subsequently stumbled when reaching to open the front passenger door. By then, three attendees of the comic book convention grabbed and pulled the man down. Others joined a growing pile – one was dressed as Spider-Man.

The driver declared in a gravelly voice, "Shit." He decided to give up on his comrades, slipped the van into drive, and hit the accelerator. He drove for less than 25 yards before being closed in by two police cars that had been parked on the other side of the arena. The front doors of the patrol cars opened, and an officer with a drawn gun emerged from each. One officer ordered, "Hands, I want to see your hands."

At the same time, a young man climbed out of the pile announcing, "Hey, look, we got his gun. We did it."

Grant turned to Kelly, who was now sitting up. He asked, "Are you alright?"

In a shaky voice, she answered, "Yes, I think so. Thank you so much."

Grant then looked around in amazement. To his right, a faux Wonder Woman stood with a boot on a kidnapper lying prone on the ground. To his left, Hawkman was pointing his mace at another man face down on the cement. Ahead of him, six comic book fans now kept another kidnapper at bay by simply sitting on him. And the police moved in and pulled the driver out of the van. For good measure, the man under Grant wasn't going anywhere.

To make the entire scene even more surreal, from behind came a roar. Grant turned his head, and saw hundreds of people from the convention standing not that far away. They were cheering and clapping.

Standing in front was Zack, next to a mystified Jed Raft.

Pushing his way through the crowd came Wes Jenkins, who ran to his wife, and hugged her.

Chapter 14

More than an hour after saving Kelly Jenkins, Stephen watched as two police detectives approached Drake Werth.

Drake had been sitting – staring and mumbling – behind the J&H Comics tables since people had streamed outside to see the foiling of a kidnapping. People passing by heard him muttering, "She hated me. She said I should die and get out of the way. Why?"

Now, the police were doing the talking. Stephen didn't have to hear the exact words. He knew what was occurring. Werth was being read his rights, and arrested for being behind the attempted kidnapping of Kelly Jenkins.

Zack arrived next to Stephen, and asked, "So, what exactly was this about?"

Stephen replied, "I spoke with Wes and one of the detectives. Two of the kidnappers sang with the promise of some kind of deal. Apparently, the team was hired by Werth."

"What was he trying to achieve?"

"He knew that if Wes walked away with all of his characters, J&H would be finished. Werth sank all of his money into buying Simon Huck's half of the business. He thought he could convince or force Wes to go along with taking the company's publications in a different direction. But once Wes published his piece in *The Wall Street Journal*, Werth was too stupid to follow Wes' lead. So, in the end, he was staring at financial ruin. The plan that he and the lead kidnapper hatched was to kidnap Kelly. They'd threaten her life, and tell Wes that he had to keep it quiet and sign over all of his characters to J&H."

"But then what? Afterwards, Wes and Kelly simply would have turned in Werth and the kidnappers to the police."

Grant looked Zack in the eyes, and shook his head. "After getting Wes' signature, no one would hear from Kelly or Wes ever again."

Zack took a gulp and only responded by saying, "Oh." He paused, and then added, "Seems dicey, at best. Did he really think he'd get away with it?"

"Good question. The detective told me that one of the guys who sang said that the lead kidnapper recognized Werth's desperation. All the kidnappers needed was to pull off the kidnapping, get the signature and get rid of the bodies. Then they'd get paid, and quite nicely, and leave the country. They would get away, and ultimately, they could not care less what would happen to Werth."

They stood in silence as Werth was led away in handcuffs. Werth was mumbling, "Yes, yes, of course."

Zack commented, "Well, no one is going to ever forget this comic con."

"True," replied Stephen.

The two men stood in silence for a couple of minutes.

Zack then said, "By the way, I managed to catch a bit of you in action, along with Hawkman and Wonder Woman."

"Did you?"

"Impressive. If you ever decided to do something other than being a parish pastor, I think you could be a spy or something." He knowingly smiled.

"Thanks. I'll keep that in mind."

Chapter 15

On Monday morning, Zack and Stephen returned to the Suffolk Arena. During the previous evening, they told Wes and Kelly that they'd swing by to say good-bye.

Joined by Diego Delarosa and Tara Tower, Wes and Kelly had the merchandise tables nearly packed up when Stephen and Zack approached.

Stephen asked Wes, "So, what's the plan now? Are you still going ahead with the new publishing house or going to salvage J&H?"

"Kelly and I discussed this last night, and I was able to talk on the phone with Sy."

Zack asked, "How is he?"

"He's in hospice care."

"I'm sorry."

"Thanks." Wes paused momentarily, and then continued, "Sy agreed with us that we should let J&H close, and move on to a new venture."

Zack and Stephen nodded in response.

Wes added, "I told him that the new company will carry the name Huck & Jenkins Comics." His voice shook a bit, and Kelly came over and put her arm around him.

The conversation eventually turned to looking ahead. While Stephen enjoyed listening to Wes, Kelly, Diego and Tara excitedly talking about their next steps with characters and ideas for new titles, Zack seemed to be taken away by the conversation.

During the good-byes, Zack exchanged cell numbers and email addresses with each person now working at Huck & Jenkins, with Stephen then doing the same.

The Jenkins pledged to visit St. Mary's when back in the area.

Before Wes climbed behind the steering wheel of a now fully-packed van, he shook hands with and thanked Zack one more time. He then turned to Stephen, and said, "I've been talking with Zack about what you've done here over the last few days. He also filled me in a bit more on your background, before becoming a pastor."

"Did he?" replied Stephen, glancing at Zack as well.

Wes continued, "He did. A former Navy SEAL, and you were with the CIA."

Stephen merely nodded.

"And now a pastor. Stephen, you sound like a great character for one of our new titles."

Stephen laughed at that.

Wes smiled, and said, "I'm serious."

"Thanks, Wes. I think." Grant then looked him in the eyes, and added, "I hope you wouldn't. It could create issues for me."

Wes paused, and said, "Your call, Stephen. No problem."

Stephen smiled and said, "Thanks."

Wes got in the vehicle, and lowered the window. "But, if you ever think it would be fun to have a Stephen Grant-like character in the comics, let me know."

Grant shook his hand, and said, "You'll be the first one I contact." He took a step back, but then added, "Hey, wait. I forgot about something. A friend at the FBI was looking for the issue of the *Avengers* where Captain America returns."

Wes said, "*Avengers #4.*"

"Right. At the Bureau, they call this agent Captain America."

"I have three copies of that issue, and I'd be glad to send him one."

Stephen smiled. "That would be great. How much do we owe you?"

"It's on me. The very least I can do. Email me his address."

"But he said it was expensive."

"No buts."

"Okay. Thank you." Stephen paused, and added, "Fight the good fight, Wes."

Wes looked back and forth between Zack and Stephen. He nodded, and said, "Keep the faith." He then raised the window, and drove away.

Chapter 16

Nearly two weeks after the convention, on a Friday night, Jennifer and Stephen were cleaning up dishes after dinner.

Jennifer asked, "So, what's the deal with you and a new car? Have you decided anything?"

"As a matter of fact, I have."

"Okay, so are you going to let me in on this?"

Stephen glanced at the clock on the wall. "Yes, any minute now."

"What does that mean?"

"Hawkman and Wonder Woman are due any minute."

"Excuse me?"

"You know, Guy and Diane. The couple at the comic convention."

"Yes, you told me all about them and how they helped you do battle with evildoers." She smiled.

"Well, I didn't tell you everything about..."

The doorbell rang.

"Perfect," commented Stephen, as he started toward the front door.

"Stephen, what's going on?"

As he walked, Stephen spoke quickly, "Guy and Diane have their own auto restoration business. And I picked out a car. That's them with it now."

As she followed, Jennifer asked, "Why all of the secrecy?"

"You'll see."

Stephen opened the door, and welcomed the Nodells into the house. Introductions were made, and Stephen and Jennifer invited the couple to take a quick tour of the house.

Diane commented, “You have a lovely home.”

“Thank you,” responded Jennifer.

After a brief pause, Guy asked, “Okay, are you two ready?”

Stephen said, “I am, but Jennifer is in the dark.”

Guy said, “That’s awesome that you were able to keep this secret.”

“Thanks.”

Jennifer looked at her husband, raised an eyebrow, and said, “Stephen.”

“Right, it’s time. Come on.”

The four stopped at the closed front door. Guy, Diane and Stephen were beaming. And then Stephen opened the door.

Jennifer stepped outside and saw the car that the Nodells had delivered. It was a red 1957 Thunderbird with its top down. Jennifer stood still and put a hand over her mouth.

Guy asked, “This is the one, right? Stephen said that growing up you were a big fan of the TV show *Vega$* with Robert Urich.”

Jennifer still didn’t move or reply.

Diane explained, “And this is the car he drove in the show. Well, not the exact car, but you know what I mean.”

Jennifer took her hand down, and revealed a giddy smile. “Oh, my God. Thank you so much.” She hugged Diane and then Guy.

Guy said, “You’re welcome. But we just upgraded the engine and restored a few things. This was all Stephen’s idea.”

Jennifer said, “I know. I know.” She walked over to Stephen, and wrapped her arms around his neck. She kissed him, and then said, “I can’t believe you did this. Thanks so much.”

“You’re welcome, Jen. I love you.”

“And I love you, too.”

She turned and moved to the car, proceeding to soak it all in.

Stephen added, "I'm pretty sure that I owed you big time after wrecking three of our cars in recent years, including, of course, your first Thunderbird."

Jennifer said, "You sure did."

Everyone laughed.

Stephen couldn't resist saying, "So, which car are you driving, this one or the Jeep?"

Jennifer smiled, and said, "Enjoy your Jeep."

Stephen nodded. "I kind of figured that." He looked at Guy and Diane, and said, "She never lets me drive her car. So, I'm finally getting behind the wheel of a nice Jeep."

Guy asked Jennifer, "And what about this Thunderbird? Will Stephen be driving this at all?"

"We'll see."

Stephen said, "That's not a 'no.'"

Jennifer slipped into the driver's seat, adding, "Don't get your hopes up. It's not a 'yes,' either."

Stephen smiled at his wife's joy and sense of humor.

Jennifer then announced, "But I do think that you deserve to join me for the first drive, my love."

As Stephen settled into the passenger seat, Jennifer looked at Guy and Diane, and asked, "Do you guys mind waiting for a few minutes while we take a quick spin, and then we'll go inside for a celebration?"

"Sounds wonderful," said Diane. "Enjoy the car."

Jennifer replied, "We will. And by the way, Stephen was right. You two really are superheroes."

Acknowledgments

Thank you to the members of the Pastor Stephen Grant Fellowship for their support:

Ultimate Readers
Jody Baran

Bronze Readers
Michelle Behl
Tyrel Bramwell
Mike Eagle
Sue Kreft

Readers
Gregory Brown
Robert Rosenberg

As always, thanks to Beth for her love, edits and insights. I also thank my two sons, David and Jonathan, for their love and support, and for their enjoyment of comics and superheroes.

Thanks to The Reverend Tyrel Bramwell for creating the cover for this book. Shortcomings in my books, of course, are always about me.

I appreciate that so many people have invested in not only purchasing and reading my books, but also in providing encouragement. Thanks.

As long as someone keeps reading, I'll keep writing. God bless.

Ray Keating
April 2018

About the Author

This is Ray Keating's first Pastor Stephen Grant short story, but the ninth entry in the overall Pastor Stephen Grant series. The first eight novels are *Warrior Monk*, followed by *Root of All Evil?*, *An Advent for Religious Liberty*, *The River*, *Murderer's Row*, *Wine Into Water*, *Lionhearts*, and *Reagan Country*.

Keating also is an author of various nonfiction books, an economist, and a podcaster. In addition, he is a columnist with RealClearMarkets.com, and a former weekly columnist for *Newsday*, *Long Island Business News*, and the *New York City Tribune*. His work has appeared in a wide range of additional periodicals, including *The New York Times, The Wall Street Journal, The Washington Post, New York Post,* Los Angeles *Daily News, The Boston Globe, National Review, The Washington Times, Investor's Business Daily,* New York *Daily News, Detroit Free Press, Chicago Tribune, Providence Journal Bulletin, TheHill.com, Touchstone* magazine, *Townhall.com, Newsmax,* and *Cincinnati Enquirer*. Keating lives on Long Island with his family.

Enjoy All of the Pastor Stephen Grant Novels!

Paperbacks and Kindle versions at Amazon.com

Signed books at raykeatingonline.com

• ***Reagan Country: A Pastor Stephen Grant Novel* by Ray Keating**

Could President Ronald Reagan's influence reach into the former "evil empire"? The media refers to a businessman on the rise as "Russia's Reagan." Unfortunately, others seek a return to the old ways, longing for Russia's former "greatness." The dispute becomes deadly. Conflict stretches from the Reagan Presidential Library in California to the White House to a Russian Orthodox monastery to the Kremlin. Stephen Grant, pastor at St. Mary's Lutheran Church on Long Island, a former Navy SEAL and onetime CIA operative, stands at the center of the tumult.

• ***Lionhearts: A Pastor Stephen Grant Novel* by Ray Keating**

War has arrived on American soil, with Islamic terrorists using new tactics. Few are safe, including Christians, politicians, and the media. Pastor Stephen Grant taps into his past with the Navy SEALS and the CIA to help wage a war of flesh and blood, ideas, history, and beliefs. This is about defending both the U.S. and Christianity.

• ***Wine Into Water: A Pastor Stephen Grant Novel*** **by Ray Keating**

Blood, wine, sin, justice and forgiveness… Who knew the wine business could be so sordid and violent? That's what happens when it's infiltrated by counterfeiters. A pastor, once a Navy SEAL and CIA operative, is pulled into action to help unravel a mystery involving fake wine, murder and revenge. Stephen Grant is called to take on evil, while staying rooted in his life as a pastor.

• ***Murderer's Row: A Pastor Stephen Grant Novel*** **by Ray Keating**

How do rescuing a Christian family from the clutches of Islamic terrorists, minor league baseball in New York, a string of grisly murders, sordid politics, and a pastor, who once was a Navy SEAL and CIA operative, tie together? *Murderer's Row* is the fifth Pastor Stephen Grant novel, and Keating serves up fascinating characters, gripping adventure, and a tangled murder mystery, along with faith, politics, humor, and, yes, baseball.

• ***The River: A Pastor Stephen Grant Novel*** **by Ray Keating**

Some refer to Las Vegas as Sin City. But the sins being committed in *The River* are not what one might typically expect. Rather, it's about murder. Stephen Grant once used lethal skills for the Navy SEALs and the CIA. Now, years later, he's a pastor. How does this man of action and faith react when his wife is kidnapped, a deep mystery must be untangled, and both allies and suspects from his CIA days arrive on the scene? How far can Grant go – or will he go –

to save the woman he loves? Will he seek justice or revenge, and can he tell the difference any longer?

• ***An Advent for Religious Liberty: A Pastor Stephen Grant Novel* by Ray Keating**

Advent and Christmas approach. It's supposed to be a special season for Christians. But it's different this time in New York City. Religious liberty is under assault. The Catholic Church has been called a "hate group." And it's the newly elected mayor of New York City who has set off this religious and political firestorm. Some people react with prayer – others with violence and murder. Stephen Grant, former CIA operative turned pastor, faces deadly challenges during what becomes known as "An Advent for Religious Liberty." Grant works with the cardinal who leads the Archdiocese of New York, the FBI, current friends, and former CIA colleagues to fight for religious liberty, and against dangers both spiritual and physical.

• ***Root of All Evil? A Pastor Stephen Grant Novel* by Ray Keating**

Do God, politics and money mix? In *Root of All Evil?*, the combination can turn out quite deadly. Keating introduced readers to Stephen Grant, a former CIA operative and current parish pastor, in the fun and highly praised *Warrior Monk*. Now, Grant is back in *Root of All Evil?* It's a breathtaking thriller involving drug traffickers, politicians, the CIA and FBI, a shadowy foreign regime, the Church, and money. Charity, envy and greed are on display. Throughout, action runs high.

• ***Warrior Monk: A Pastor Stephen Grant Novel*** **by Ray Keating**

Warrior Monk revolves around a former CIA assassin, Stephen Grant, who has lived a far different, relatively quiet life as a parish pastor in recent years. However, a shooting at his church, a historic papal proposal, and threats to the Pope's life mean that Grant's former and current lives collide. Grant must tap the varied skills learned as a government agent, a theologian and a pastor not only to protect the Pope, but also to feel his way through a minefield of personal challenges.

All of the Pastor Stephen Grant novels are available at Amazon.com and signed books at www.raykeatingonline.com.

Join the Pastor Stephen Grant Fellowship!

Visit
www.patreon.com/pastorstephengrantfellowship

Consider joining the Pastor Stephen Grant Fellowship to enjoy more of Pastor Stephen Grant and the related novels, receive new short stories, enjoy special thanks, gain access to even more content, receive special gifts, and perhaps even have a character named after you, a friend or a loved one.

Ray Keating declares, “I’ve always said that I’ll keep writing as long as someone wants to read what I write. Thanks to reader support from this Patreon effort, I will be able to pen more Pastor Stephen Grant and related novels, while also generating short stories, reader guides, and other fun material. At various levels of support, you can become an essential part of making this happen, while getting to read everything that is written before the rest of the world, and earning other exclusive benefits – some that are pretty darn cool!”

Readers can join at various levels…

- **Reader Level at $4.99 per month…**

You receive all new novels FREE and two weeks earlier than the rest of the world, and you get FREE exclusive, early reads of new Pastor Stephen Grant short stories throughout the year. In addition, your name is included in a special "Thank You" section in forthcoming novels, and you gain access to the private Pastor Stephen Grant Fellowship Facebook page, which includes daily journal entries from

Pastor Stephen Grant, insights from other characters, regular recipes from Grillin' with the Monks, periodic videos and Q&A's with Ray Keating, and more!

- **Bronze Reader Level at $9.99 per month...**

All the benefits from the above level, plus you receive two special gift boxes throughout the year with fun and exclusive Pastor Stephen Grant merchandise.

- **Silver Reader Level at $22.99 per month...**

All the benefits from the above levels, plus you receive two additional (for a total of four) special gift boxes throughout the year with fun and exclusive Pastor Stephen Grant merchandise, and you get a signed, personalized (signed to you or the person of your choice as a gift) Pastor Stephen Grant novel three times a year.

- **Gold Reader Level at $39.99 per month...**

All the benefits from the above levels, plus your name or the name of someone you choose to be used for a character in <u>one</u> upcoming novel.

- **Ultimate Reader Level at $49.99 per month...**

All the benefits from the above levels, plus your name or the name of someone you choose (in addition to the one named under the Gold level!) to be used for a <u>major recurring character</u> in upcoming novels.

Visit www.patreon.com/pastorstephengrantfellowship

Tune in to Ray Keating's Authors and Entrepreneurs Podcast

This entertaining podcast brings together authors, aspiring authors, entrepreneurs, and aspiring entrepreneurs for an exploration of the world of authors as entrepreneurs. Designed with readers and book lovers in mind, the podcast discusses the creative and business aspects of being a writer, and what that means for authors themselves as well as for the reading public. Keating interviews interesting guests, and serves up assorted insights and ideas.

Listen in and subscribe at iTunes, or on Buzzsprout at http://www.buzzsprout.com/147907.

Enjoy *"Chuck" vs. the Business World: Business Tips on TV* by Ray Keating

Paperback and for the Kindle at Amazon.com

Signed books at raykeatingonline.com

Ray Keating also writes nonfiction books, and his most enjoyable is *"Chuck" vs. the Business World: Business Tips on TV*. In this book, Keating finds career advice, and lessons on managing or owning a business in a fun, fascinating and unexpected place, that is, in the television show *Chuck*.

Keating shows that TV spies and nerds can provide insights and guidelines on managing workers, customer relations, leadership, technology, hiring and firing people, and balancing work and personal life. Larry Kudlow of CNBC says, "Ray Keating has taken the very funny television series *Chuck*, and derived some valuable lessons and insights for your career and business."

If you love *Chuck*, you'll love this book. And even if you never watched *Chuck*, the book lays out clear examples and quick lessons from which you can reap rewards.

Made in the USA
Lexington, KY
26 September 2018